Look in the book and find the...

pig and piglets

the horse and foal

the tractor

the cat

the ducks

the donkey

the hens

the goat

the sheep and lamb

the cow and calf

the bees

the goose

Learning Points

•

Farms and farm animals fascinate young children. Your child will enjoy
sharing *Joe and the Farm Goose* with you again and again.

•

Encourage your child to talk about the animals he or she has seen.
What were they doing? What sounds do they make?

•

Children love to recognise baby animals.
See if your child knows what the animals are called.

•

Encourage your child to turn the pages and tell
you a story of the farm visit.

•

Use our questions as a talkabout starting point,
and then think of questions of your own.

•

Can your child find the inquisitive goose throughout the book?

Ladybird books are widely available, but in case of difficulty may be ordered by post or telephone from:

Ladybird Books – Cash Sales Department Littlegate Road Paignton Devon TQ3 3BE
Telephone 01803 554761

A catalogue record for this book is available from the British Library

Published by Ladybird Books Ltd Loughborough Leicestershire UK
Ladybird Books Inc Auburn Maine 04210 USA

Copyright illustrations © Jakki Wood MCMXCV
© LADYBIRD BOOKS LTD MCMXCV
LADYBIRD and the device of a Ladybird are trademarks of Ladybird Books Ltd

Joe
and the
Farm Goose

by Geraldine Taylor & Jill Harker
illustrated by Jakki Wood

Picture
Ladybird

Mum and Dad, Sally and Ben and little Joe
arrived at Manor Farm.

"I want to go this way," said Sally.
A friendly goose did, too!

Dad lifted Ben up to see the cows in the field.

Joe was too little to look over the hedge,
so he peeped under it. The goose did, too.

Everyone wanted to see the pigs.

Joe was too small to look over the gate,
so he peeped through it. The goose did, too.

"Keep back from the tractor!" said Mum.
"What a noise."

In a quiet corner, Joe, Dad and the goose
found a duck and three fluffy ducklings.

Sally and Ben stayed close to Dad
and watched the tractor.

Joe and the goose stayed close to Mum
and found some treasure.

In the big barn, Mum and Dad and Sally and Ben
looked up high and saw some hens.

Joe looked down low and saw some tiny mice.
The goose did, too.

One of the horses in the yard had a baby foal.
Joe peeped out from behind Mum…

The goose did, too!

Then it was time to eat…

Joe didn't want to sit at the picnic table,
he wanted to sit on the grass. The goose did, too.

In the orchard there were beehives and a goat.
"Look at those apples up there," said Dad.

But all Joe and the goose could see
were Dad's knees – and the goat.

Joe couldn't reach the apples in the orchard –
but the goose could.

Sally and Ben and Joe picked lots of strawberries.
Perhaps the goose didn't like strawberries.

The farm visit was almost over.
"What an exciting day," said Dad.

Ben and Sally thought so, too –
but little Joe was asleep.

Goodbye farm. Goodbye goose…

It's our bedtime, too!

Did you find all these things?

pig and piglets

the horse and foal

the tractor

the cat

the ducks

the donkey

the hens

the goat

the sheep and lamb

the cow and calf

the bees

the goose

Picture Ladybird

Books for reading aloud with 2–6 year olds

The *Picture Ladybird* range is full of exciting stories and rhymes that are perfect to read aloud and share. There is something for everyone – animal stories, bedtime stories, rhyming stories – and lots more!

Ten titles for you to collect

WISHING MOON AGE 3+
written & illustrated by Lesley Harker

Persephone Brown wanted to be BIG. All she ever saw were feet and knees – it really wasn't on. Then one special night her wish came true. Persephone Brown just grew and grew and *GREW...*

DON'T WORRY WILLIAM AGE 3+
by Christine Morton
illustrated by Nigel McMullen

It's a sleepy dark night. A creepy dark night. A night for naughty bears to creep downstairs and have an adventure. But, going in search of biscuits to make them brave, Horace and William hear a bang–a very loud bang–an On-The-Stairs bang! Whatever can it be?

BENEDICT GOES TO THE BEACH AGE 3+
written & illustrated by Chris Demarest

It's hot in the city – *really* hot. Poor Benedict just *has* to cool off. There is only one thing for it, head for the beach – *any* beach! Deciding is the easy part – getting there is another matter altogether...

TOOT! LEARNS TO FLY AGE 3+
by Geraldine Taylor & Jill Harker
illustrated by Georgien Overwater

It's time for Toot to learn to fly, to try and zoom across the sky. First there's take off – watch it – steady! Whoops! Bump! He's not quite ready! Follow Toot's route across the sky and see if he ever *does* learn to fly!

JOE AND THE FARM GOOSE AGE 2+
by Geraldine Taylor & Jill Harker
illustrated by Jakki Wood

A perfect way to introduce young children to farmyard life. There is lots to see and talk about – pigs and their piglets, cows and sheep, hens in the barn – and Joe's special friend – a very inquisitive goose!

THE STAR THAT FELL AGE 3+
by Karen Hayles
illustrated by Cliff Wright

When a star falls from the night sky, Fox and all the other animals want its precious warmth and brightness. When Dog finds the star he gives it to his friend Maddy. But as Maddy's dad tells her, all stars belong to the sky, and soon she must give it back.

TELEPHONE TED AGE 3+
by Joan Stimson
illustrated by Peter Stevenson

When Charlie starts playgroup poor Ted is left sitting at home like a stuffed toy. It's not much fun being a teddy on your own with no one to talk to. But then – *brring, brring* – the telephone rings, and that's when Ted's adventure begins.

JASPER'S JUNGLE JOURNEY AGE 3+
written & illustrated by Val Biro

What's behind those rugged rocks? A lion wearing purple socks! Just one of the strange sights Jasper encounters as he goes in search of his lost teddy bear. A delightful rhyming story full of jungle surprises!

SHOO FLY SHOO! AGE 4+
by Brian Moses
illustrated by Trevor Dunton

If a fly flies by and it's bothering you, just swish it and swash it and tell it to *shoo!* Trace the trail of the buzzing, zuzzing fly in this gloriously silly rhyming story.

GOING TO PLAYGROUP AGE 2+
by Geraldine Taylor & Jill Harker
illustrated by Terry McKenna

Tom's day at playgroup is full of exciting activities. He's a cook, a mechanic, a pirate and a band leader... he even flies to the moon! Ideal for children starting playgroup and full of ideas for having fun at home, too!